# What You See
# Is What You Get

Modern Curriculum Press
BEGINNING
TO
READ
Series

# What You See
# Is What You Get

### Valjean McLenighan
#### Illustrated by Dev Appleyard

MODERN CURRICULUM PRESS

ISBN: 0-8136-5584-6
Printed in the United States of America

12  13  14  15  16  17      06  05  04  03  02

Modern
Curriculum
Press

Pearson Learning Group

1-800-321-3106
www.pearsonlearning.com

7

8

9

11

13

14

15

21

22

25

Come one,
come all!
Come and see
my new things.

29

30